DISNEY'S MULAN

Adapted by Gina Ingoglia
Drawings by José Cardona
Painted by Don Williams

A GOLDEN BOOK • NEW YORK

Golden Books Publishing Company, Inc., New York, New York 10106

© 1998 Disney Enterprises, Inc. All rights reserved. Printed in the U.S.A. No part of this book may be reproduced or copied in any form without written permission from the copyright owner. A LITTLE GOLDEN BOOK®, A GOLDEN BOOK®, G DESIGN™, and the distinctive gold spine are trademarks of Golden Books Publishing Company, Inc. Library of Congress Catalog Card Number: 97-76889 ISBN: 0-307-98861-9   A MCMXCVIII First Edition 1998

ike a powerful dragon, the Great Wall of China winds across the land. It protects the country's farmland and villages, its family temples, and miles of bright green rice paddies. Along the wall, soldiers stand guard. Little do they suspect that this great barrier is about to be crossed by an army of Huns led by the ferocious Shan-Yu.

One afternoon, a young woman named Mulan sadly returned home from the village. Making a good marriage was the way a young Chinese woman brought honor to her family, but Mulan's meeting with the Matchmaker that morning had ended in disaster.

Her father, Fa Zhou, sat with her. With kind, loving words he assured his daughter that, like the late-blooming blossom that will be the most beautiful of all, she, too, would bring honor to the family.

BOOM! BOOM! BOOM! Suddenly, a loud drum was heard, summoning the people out of their homes.

"The Huns have invaded China!" a messenger announced. "One man from each family must serve in the Imperial Army."

When the Fa family was called, Fa Zhou handed his cane to his wife and stepped forward.

"No, Father!" cried Mulan. She knew her father was as brave as he had been in his youth, but he was no longer strong. He would never be able to survive a war.

It rained hard that night. Mulan went to the family temple, lit some incense, and prayed to her Ancestors.

She had made her decision. "I will take Father's place," she said.

Mulan took Fa Zhou's sword and cut her hair short. Then she put on his armor. Disguised as a man, she rode her horse, Khan, into the storm.

A tiny dragon named Mushu soon raced after her. He wanted to regain his position as a Guardian of the Fa family. "I'll make Mulan a hero! That'll show the Ancestors!" he said.

A cricket named Cri-Kee hopped along beside him. "I know I can help," he chirped. "I'm a lucky cricket."

Mulan wasn't sure what to think when Mushu and Cri-Kee first showed up. But she knew she needed all the help she could get.

When Mulan reached the army camp, she reported to Captain Shang. Shang was the son of General Li, leader of the Emperor's army. It was Shang's job to train the new recruits to be good soldiers.

"What's your name?" Shang asked.

Mulan made up a boy's name. "Ping . . ." she stuttered. "My name is Ping."

The recruits had trouble with all of the training exercises.

The most difficult test was retrieving an arrow from the top of a tall pole. No recruit had been able to do it. Finally, Mulan cleverly figured out how to use strength and discipline to get the arrow.

Everyone cheered. They would all learn to be good soldiers.

But one evening, Mushu and Cri-Kee overheard Chi Fu, the Emperor's aide, talking to Shang. "I will report to your father that your men are not fit to be soldiers," he said.

"We can't let him do that," said Mushu. "How will I make Mulan a hero if she never goes to battle?"

So Cri-Kee "typed" out a note and they delivered it to Chi Fu.

"Captain Li Shang: You and your men are needed at the front at once!" the note said.

Shang set out immediately with his troops. Soon they came
across a burned-out village that had been attacked by the Huns.

Shang was handed a helmet. It was his father's. His heart was heavy
with sadness, but he had to face his responsibilities.

"We must go to the Imperial City," he said. "We are the Emperor's
only hope."

The men trudged on.

Suddenly, hundreds of flaming arrows flew down at them. Then, out of nowhere, Shan-Yu's Hun army charged at Shang and his men.

"Fire the cannons!" yelled Shang. Soon only one cannon was left.

Mulan looked up at the snowy mountain peak and got an idea. She grabbed the last cannon and fired. It slammed into the mountain and shook the snow loose. An avalanche thundered down and swept the enemy away!

Mulan leapt on Khan and raced him across the snow to Shang, who lay unconscious. Quickly, she lifted him onto the horse's strong back. Khan skidded dangerously on the steep slope, but the other soldiers helped pull them to safety.

When Shang came to, he noticed that Mulan had been wounded. She was taken to the medic's tent.

Later, the army medic reported startling news: "This soldier isn't a man—she's a woman!" It was a crime punishable by death.

"You deceived me," Shang angrily told Mulan. "I will spare your life because you saved mine."

The troops marched off, leaving Mulan behind with Khan, Mushu, and Cri-Kee.

Mulan was about to head home in disgrace. But from the top of a cliff she saw Shan-Yu and five of his soldiers heading toward the Imperial City. They were still alive!

Mulan galloped off to the city. There she found Shang and told him that the Huns were on their way.

"You lied once," Shang said. "Why should I believe you now?"

But later, during the victory ceremony, Shan-Yu captured the Emperor. Mulan saw Shang frantically trying to break into the palace.

"I have an idea how we can get in," she called out to Shang.

Mulan dressed her three soldier friends, Yao, Ling, and Chien-Po, in women's clothes so that they could fool the Hun guards. Shang followed them, and they quickly overpowered the guards.

On a palace balcony, Shan-Yu waved his sword at the Emperor. "Bow to me!" he demanded.

At Mulan's signal, the rescuers stormed into the room.

The Emperor was taken to safety. Shan-Yu was furious. He charged
at Mulan.

She ran in search of Mushu. "Quick," she told him. "I have a
plan." She sent him and Cri-Kee off to the fireworks tower.

Mulan ran through the palace, making sure that Shan-Yu was
following her. Then she led him onto the roof.

Mushu landed on the roof. He had a rocket tied to his back. Cri-Kee lit the fuse. The rocket crashed right into Shan-Yu. Mushu jumped off, but the rocket carried Shan-Yu away toward the fireworks tower.

KABOOM! A spectacular fireworks explosion dazzled the city.

Shan-Yu was no more.

The Emperor bowed to Mulan. He gave her Shan-Yu's sword and placed his pendant around her neck. "You are a hero," he said. "You have brought great honor to your country and family." Then the Emperor asked Mulan to join his council. But Mulan chose to return to her parents, instead.

Soon, Mulan was at home, enjoying a joyous reunion with her family, when Shang arrived.

He had realized that Mulan was a very special person, indeed.

"Would you like to stay for dinner?" Mulan asked him.

Mushu was ready to celebrate. He was a Guardian once more. "Send out for egg rolls!" he cried.